Birdhouse For Rent

Harriet Ziefert

Paintings by Donald Dreifuss

HOUGHTON MIFFLIN COMPANY
BOSTON 2001

Walter Lorraine Books

For Max and Olivia
—D. D.

Walter Lorraine *wn* Books

Text copyright © 2001 by Harriet Ziefert
Illustrations copyright © 2001 by Donald Dreifuss

www.houghtonmifflinbooks.com

Library of Congress Cataloging-in-Publication Data

Ziefert, Harriet
    Birdhouse for rent / by Harriet Ziefert ; illustrated by Donald Dreifuss.
        p. cm.
    Summary: Uses the perspective of a birdhouse to depict two chickadees building a nest
        inside and raising their babies.
    ISBN 0-618-04881-2
    1. Chickadees—Juvenile fiction. [1. Chickadees—Fiction. 2. Birdhouses—Fiction.] I.
        Dreifuss, Donald, ill. II. Title.

    PZ10.3.Z45 Bi 2001
    [E]—dc21
                                                                99-045403

Printed in China for Harriet Ziefert, Inc.
HZI 10 9 8 7 6 5 4 3 2 1

I am a birdhouse.

I was put in the ground at the beginning of July.
As you can see, I am vacant. I have no tenants.

All summer, lots of birds flew over my roof. Some
even stopped to rest. I was sure the bluebird who
landed on my perch would come in, but he did not.
A starling poked his beak in my doorway,
but he didn't step inside.

Finally, in September, I had tenants.
They were wasps!

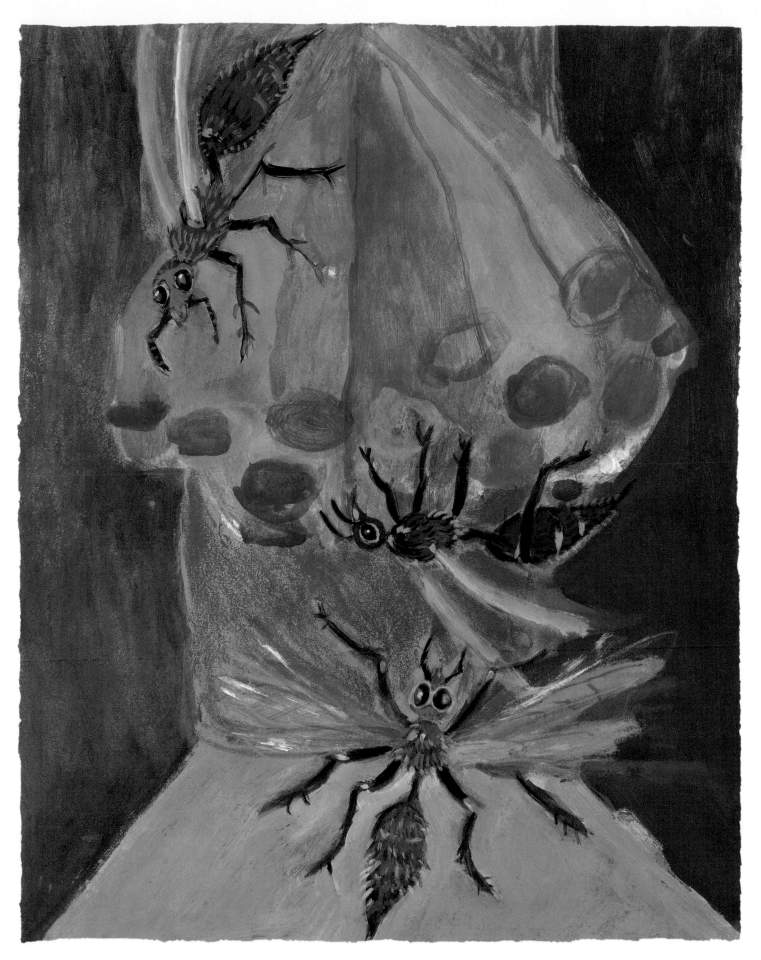

I could hear the wasps hum as they built a paper nest on my ceiling. Just look at it. It's amazing!

In October, when the weather
got cold, the wasps left.
Chipmunks moved in.
Oh, what messy tenants!

The chipmunks dragged in
leaves, grass, sticks, and more
acorns than I could count.

After a few weeks, I was ready
for the chipmunks to leave,
but they stayed all winter.

November was blowy.   **In December, it rained a lot.**

January was icy.   Heavy snow fell in February.

Unfortunately, a March storm
snapped my post.

Fortunately, the chipmunks vacated.

In early April, a farmer put me on top of a new post.
A few house-hunting birds stopped by but didn't stay.

One day a chickadee peeked
into my doorway. He hopped
all over my roof and examined me
from all angles. He seemed to find
everything to his liking.

He called to another bird,
who was perched on a nearby branch.
I thought, *That must be Mrs. Chickadee.*
She came right over.
She saw the place was snug and dry;
the entrance was well above the floor,
better for keeping out wind, rain, and enemies.
She seemed pleased.

And so they moved in!

At first, Mr. and Mrs. Chickadee spent most of their days out of the house finding insects. But after a week or two, she stayed close to home and he did the food-collecting.

Mrs. Chickadee was building a nest!

After three days of hard work, Mrs. Chickadee nestled down. The next morning, I heard Mr. Chickadee calling softly.

Mrs. Chickadee gave him an eager welcome but
did not get up. When she arched her back to reach
for a nice, juicy caterpillar, I saw an egg!

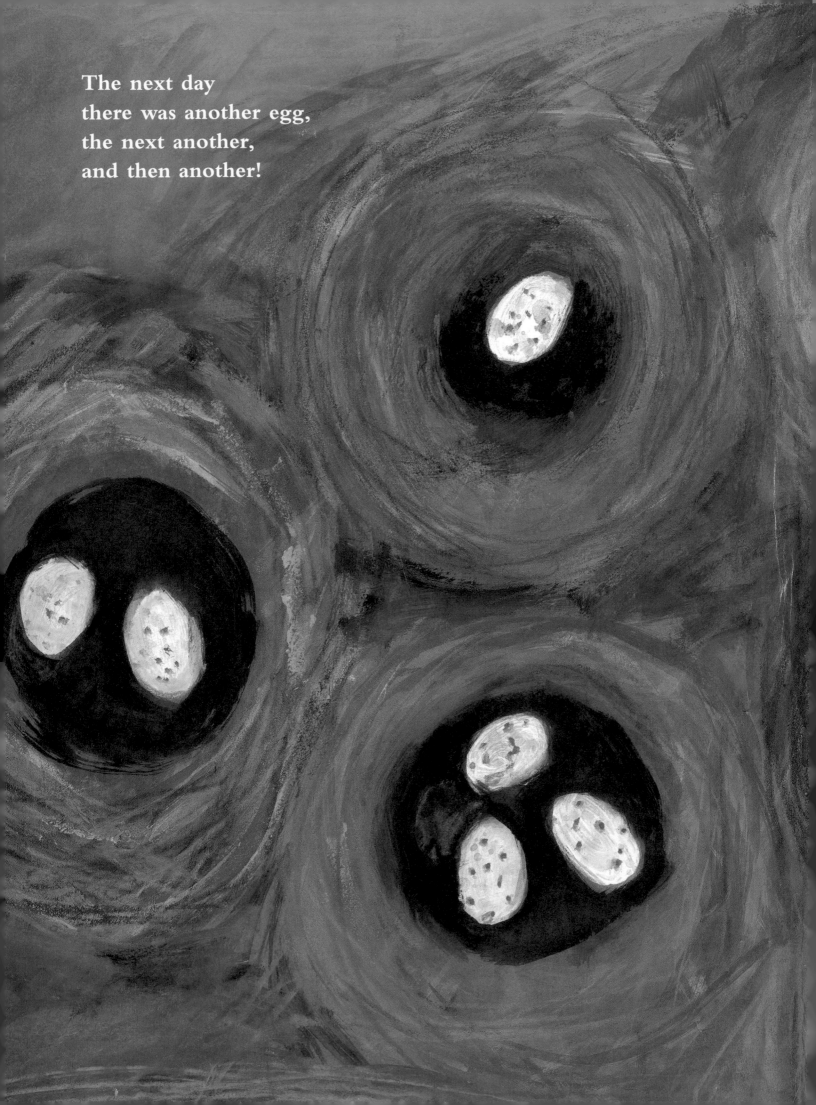

The next day
there was another egg,
the next another,
and then another!

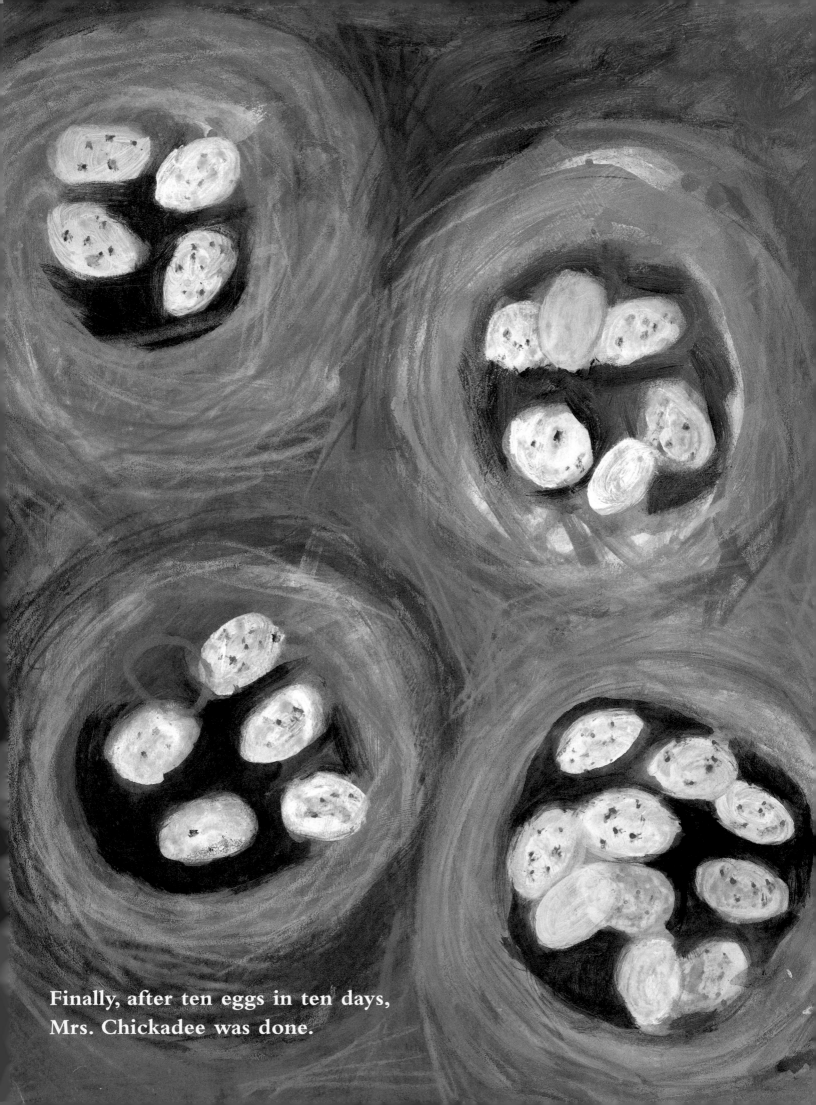

Finally, after ten eggs in ten days,
Mrs. Chickadee was done.

For weeks, Mrs. Chickadee had been spending nearly all
of her time inside the house. Now she stayed outside
all day, leaving her eggs deserted. But she did cover them
before she flew off, so an egg thief wouldn't eat them.

Unfortunately, the farmer's cat was too smart
for Mrs. Chickadee, and I watched him steal three
of her eggs.

Finally, the eggs started to hatch.
After two days, there were seven baby birds.

The babies always had their mouths wide open, begging
to be fed. All together, I counted 600 feedings a day!

When the babies were a few days old,
the cat returned, looking for more to eat.

Mr. and Mrs. Chickadee made a lot of noise and chased him away. The babies were safe!

As the babies grew, the place became quite
crowded. I could hear little cheeps all day long,
as if the babies were saying, *When can we go outside?*

And they did...in early June, when they were big and plump and could fly! They came in and out for a few days, then they left my house completely.

I wonder who the next tenants will be.